This Walker book
belongs to:

The Bus Is

Michael Rosen

For Emma, Elsie and Emile... M.R.   ✳ ∿ ✳   *For Frazer McGown love Aunty Gilly*

First published 2015 by Walker Books Ltd, 87 Vauxhall Walk, London SE11 5HJ ◆ This edition published 2016 ◆ Text © 2015 Michael Rosen ◆ Illustrations © 2015 Gillian Tyler ◆ The right of Michael Rosen and Gillian Tyler to be identified as author and illustrator respectively of this work has been asserted by them in accordance with the Copyright, Designs and Patents Act 1988 ◆ This book has been typeset in AT Arta ◆ Printed in China ◆ All rights reserved.

For Us!

Gillian Tyler

WALKER BOOKS

AND SUBSIDIARIES

LONDON • BOSTON • SYDNEY • AUCKLAND

I really like
to ride my bike

I like going far

in our car

YR2APY

When it

starts to rain

I like
the train.

But best is the bus.
The bus is for us.

I do of course
like riding a horse

I like to float

in a little boat

I like trips
in big ships.

But best is the bus.

**The bus
is for us.**

Sometimes I wish
I could ride on a fish

If I was allowed
I'd sit on a cloud

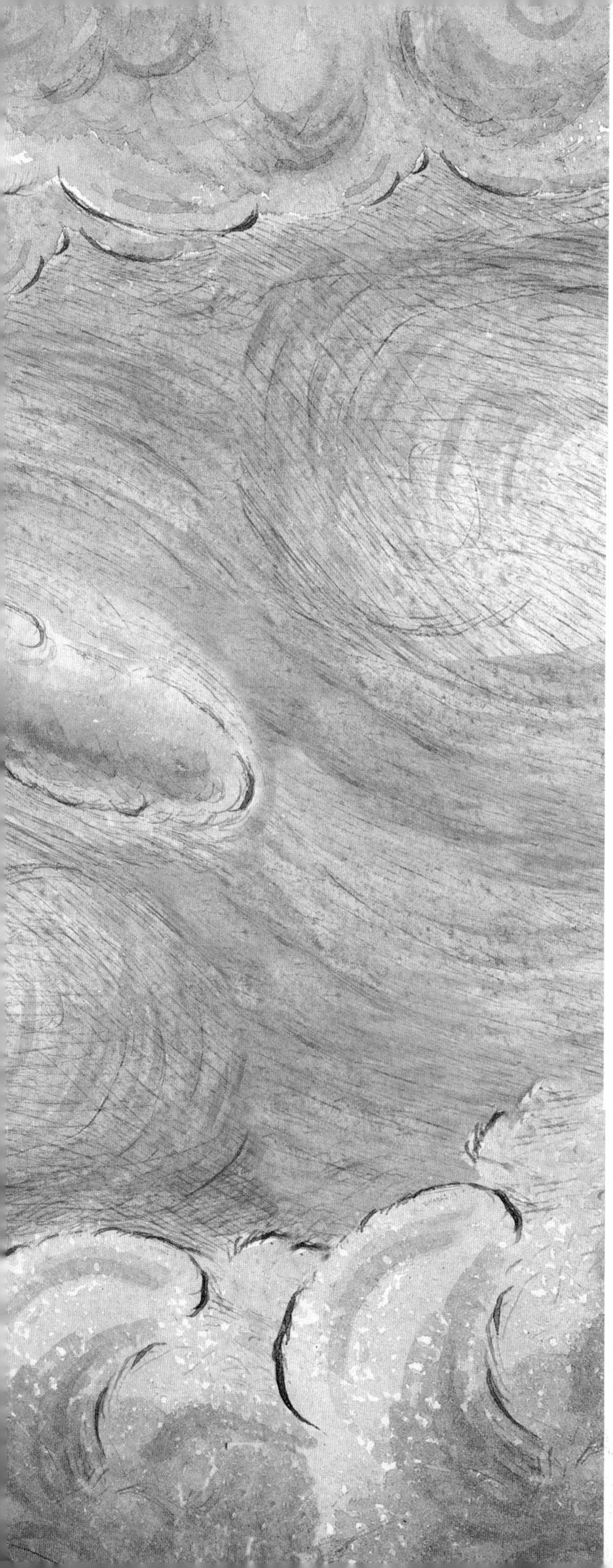

I'd be all right
up high on a kite.

But best is the bus.
The bus is for us.

I'd love to play

in an open sleigh

Fly to the moon
in a hot-air balloon

Or for a dare
ride on a bear.

But even so

the bus is best.

Best is the bus.

That's because

**the bus
is for US!**

Also by Michael Rosen and Gillian Tyler

978-0-7445-2323-2

978-1-4063-0379-7

978-1-4063-4319-9

Available from all good booksellers

www.walker.co.uk